MW00334873

LAST DAYS OF

John Brown,

THE ABOLITIONIST

LAST DAYS OF

John Brown,

THE ABOLITIONIST

A Short Story

Second Edition

Doris N. Starks

ISBN: 978-1-64826-542-6   (Paperback Edition)
ISBN: 978-1-64826-543-3   (Hardcover Edition)
ISBN: 978-1-64826-541-9   (E-book Edition)

Some characters and events in this book are fictitious. Any similarity to real persons, living or dead, is coincidental and not intended by the author.

Book Ordering Information

Phone Number: 347-901-4929 or 347-901-4920
Email: info@globalsummithouse.com
Global Summit House
www.globalsummithouse.com

Printed in the United States of America

John Brown

It was October 22, 1859, six days after his raid on Harpers Ferry, and John Brown, the abolitionist, stirred uncomfortably on his cot in the jail in Charlestown, Virginia. He rubbed his bleary eyes and tried to clear the fog in his brain as he struggled to remember the events that brought him to this Godforsaken place.

Brown ached all over as his wounds begged for relief. There were three stab wounds in his body, and a slash across his

1

chest. Maybe it would help to clear his head and put things in order if he could just start from the beginning. Then he could begin to figure a way out of this awful mess in which he had gotten himself and others.

Owen Brown

He was born on May 9, 1800, to Owen and Ruth Brown in Torrington, Connecticut.

When he was five years old, his father moved his family to Ohio, where his dad operated a tannery.

The 59-year-old man remembered that his father, Owen, brought his family up under the precepts of the Congregational Church, which had members who often spoke out on the need for human rights for all people. He thought about how he even had hopes in his early years of becoming a Congregational minister.

The tired, aging man recalled that in his younger years, when he served on Oberlin Collegiate Institute's Board of Trustees, 1835 to 1844, he had an opportunity to survey and scout the western mountainous area of Virginia. It was called the Gerrit Smith Oberlin Virginia Lands. That's when he became familiar with the area around Harpers Ferry. He got a good look at the steep mountains with rippling brooks that led to rivers. He also saw the dense underbrush and trees. Flowers grew out of the most unlikely places and birds chirped all the time. In October, the month in which the raid just happened to take place, you could count on the trees to be at their peak, seeing which one could outdo the other; showing all shades of gold, orange, rust, and red. Harpers Ferry was really a beautiful town, nestled in a valley with mountains surrounding it.

Brown recalled that he married his first wife, Dianthe Luske in 1820. They had seven children, and Dianthe died in 1832, shortly after giving birth. The following year, 1833, he married 16-year-old Mary Ann Day and they had an additional 13 children together, although only six lived to be adults.

Vivid scenes involving the friends he made after moving most of his family to Springfield, Massachusetts, pushed their way into Brown's mind. While in Springfield he felt most comfortable among those who were downtrodden and were considered 'underdogs.' When he attended lectures at the Sanford Street Free Church he heard abolitionists like Frederick Douglass and Sojourner Truth speak passionately about their experiences as slaves and the need to liberate others from such soul destroying lives. He even met Harriet Tubman who told of her own efforts as a Conductor on the Underground Railroad to rescue many from bondage. To hear of their exploits made him even more convinced that he should dedicate himself to ensuring that all men, women and children should live free, like God intended them to be.

Brown recalled that in 1848, he relocated some of his family to upstate New York, near North Elba, where Gerrit Smith was offering land grants to poor Black families for $1.00 per acre. Since his sentiments were with poor, struggling, Black families, he thought he might as well live among them.

Swirling thoughts caused Brown to remember that most of his family members were in New York, while some of his adult sons and their families were living in Kansas. He remembered how his sons had told him of pro-slavery attacks and uprisings. Since he was determined to protect his sons, their families, and others against the pro-slavery settlers, he went to Kansas with a small band of men. While he was there, Brown's men were said to have killed five men. But Brown denied having killed anyone, although he acknowledged giving approval for the operation.

As a large roach crawled along the ceiling of his cell, Brown's blood seethed when he recalled that in 1850, the nation passed the Fugitive Slave Act which further infuriated him. The law required authorities in free states to assist in the return of escaped slaves to their masters. There were penalties for those who might be found guilty of helping slaves to escape. Brown thought, "Has this country lost its collective mind?"

He even thought of how that fool of a Supreme Court Chief Justice, Roger Taney, of Maryland, writing for the majority in the Dred Scott V. Standford case (1857), held that Scott, a slave, was not entitled to rights as a citizen, because he was the property of his master. That is, a slave could not vote or sue in court because of his status. That ruling made Brown hot under the collar, as it did many other abolitionists. Brown was sure it would not lead to a good end. It would only further divide the nation. Not only that, it could even lead to war! People were calling him hot-headed, but what could those slave-holders and people who supported them be thinking? Were not all people equal in the sight of God?

As he lay there, Brown pondered how the founding fathers must have viewed the question of slavery. Some must have considered it essential for the growth and development of the new nation. Then, there was George Mason IV, a delegate to the Constitutional Convention from Virginia in 1787. Although Mason owned slaves, he argued vehemently against the continued importation of slaves into the country from Africa. Further, he was against the spread of slavery to states which were not already characterized as slave-holding ones. Mason was so displeased with the draft of the Constitution as it related to slavery that he refused to sign the document.

Mason had made such a forceful presentation at the Constitutional Convention about the need to protect individual rights that on December 15, 1791, the Bill of Rights was added to the U. S. Constitution. It was largely based on the Declaration of Rights which Mason had written for Virginia. Mason expressed the belief that if protection was not given for individual rights it would set the stage for conflict in the future.

At the same Constitutional Convention, participants negotiated to count slaves as three- fifths of a person in order to balance power in the House of Representatives among southern and northern states. Northerners were willing to settle for this compromise in order to get southerners to ratify the constitution, or they would not sign it.

Although the idea of slaves being only three-fifths of a person was demeaning in and of itself, it was the only way, many thought, to get unity on the matter. On the other hand when one compared the body of a slave, or any other body regardless of color, to a nation, what three-fifths could it do without? What body system could it function without? A body needs its whole, healthy self to function appropriately! This was sure to cause trouble in the future.

As he pondered these things, Brown thought he knew why some people called George Mason an abolitionist before he, John, came along. On reflection, John Brown thought it was a worthy cause to be an abolitionist, and welcomed anyone to join who was willing to make the sacrifice.

He thought further of his friend, Harriet Tubman. She had made 19 trips into Southern Maryland to lead over 300 people to freedom without losing a single one of them. She had planned to come with him on his raid, but was ill when he left. Maybe if she had come her wisdom and intuition would have led his raiding party to a success and he could have made better decisions.

That Harriet was some woman. She once told John of how much she enjoyed eating apples when she was a child. She said it was her desire to plant more apple seeds so that in later years other people could enjoy eating apples. Now, wasn't that the way life was supposed to be? We do good deeds during our lifetimes to make life better for those who come after us? Harriet. So strong, but yet so sweet!

As Brown struggled to get the old musty blanket to cover all of his long body in the chill while in the too-short bed, he wondered if others who used the blanket had similar problems. Did they break out into cold sweats while pondering their fates? What became of them? What other traces of themselves did they leave on the face of this earth? Maybe he would speak to the jailer about getting the blanket laundered.

Brown thought of his well-to-do friends in Springfield who had financed his mission. They had provided money without asking too many questions. He, and others around him referred to this largely unknown cadre as the "Group of Six," or sometimes called the "Secret Six." They shared Brown's ideals, but were not as headstrong as Brown. They did not ask why he needed guns and pikes (spear-like knives on the end of long poles), but he had told the closest of this inner circle that he was planning an invasion to rescue Black people in an area where they were being held in bondage, against their will. He

8

had further informed them that there was also enough land in that area of the Appalachian mountains where a section could be set aside for a state designated for liberated slaves. He expected that with his help, many of those who were enslaved would free themselves.

Had some of this trusted "Group of Six" told too much about his plan to others, who then revealed his intent to those who could do him harm? Brown could not say. He did know, however, that they did not want their own names made public. In the stillness of his cell, Brown enumerated the names of the "Secret Six": They were; Gerrit Smith, George Steams, Thomas Wentworth, Theodore Parker, Franklin Sanborn, and Samuel Gridley Howe.

Brown thought of his fellow abolitionists who had attended the meeting he held on April 27, 1858, in Chatham, Ontario in Canada. At that convention of Blacks and Whites, a Provisional Constitution was adopted for the newly proposed state for freed slaves.

Brown remembered that although Martin Delany, a free Black physician who had helped him put the convention together, supported his efforts, he thought that Brown was somewhat rash in his thinking, and might somehow get many people killed. As Brown watched the light from the lamp in his cell make weird pictures on the wall, he felt that Delany had been prophetic, no matter how his own situation progressed. Although he respected the thinking of the physician from Charlestown, Brown knew that if slavery continued as it was going, slaves would eventually revolt and there would be bloodshed. Or, the argument between the states concerning the holding of other human beings as property and denying them their rights could only lead to major bloodshed in the form of war.

As Brown reflected on his past he became drowsy, and thought that before he went to sleep he would read some from his treasured Bible. He already knew his favorite passage by heart. It gave him solace and comfort, and could be repeated even if he did not have the book with him, or if others were present, or heaven forbid, the moment was stressful. The passage was "The Lord's Prayer," found in the 6th chapter of Matthew of the King James Version of the Bible. It read:

"Our Father, who art in heaven.
Hallowed be thy name.

Thy kingdom come. Thy will be done,
in earth, as it is In heaven....

As he closed his eyes, Brown imagined that he felt the gentle touch of his wife's hand on his, and the sweetness of her perfume as he drifted off to sleep.

The next day Brown was awakened by the clanging, banging and slamming of cell doors. The noise made his head ache, and he wondered if someone was coming to take him away. But no, it was just the opposite. A portly young man with dark hair said, "Ahem! Sorry to disturb you, Mr. Brown. My name is John Blessing. I'm a cook and a baker. I have volunteered to cook for you and your men while you're here in the Charlestown jail. I've brought you something to eat. So, if you can rouse yourself, I'll bring you a basin and water to wash yourself up a bit, then you can eat!"

That was the kindest thing anyone had said to John Brown since he had arrived in Charlestown. He responded, "I sure could use some vittles. I hope you're a good cook, but if you're not, I would not know the difference, I'm so hungry!" Then he asked if all the other members of his group were being fed and receiving care. Blessing assured him that they were. However, Blessing did not go into detail about the men who were killed in the raid. The man had already been through so much, and there was still a long way to go.

True to his word, Blessing brought the basin of water, with soap and a towel, and allowed Brown time to clean himself up as best he could. Blessing noted the wounds, but chose not to mention them on this first meeting. He would ask Brown later if he could help by dressing them for him. He knew some good home remedies and had some potions he used when he burned or cut himself in his cooking and baking business.

Brown hurriedly cared for himself, that is, as fast as his wounds would allow, because he did not want his food to get cold. When he sat down to the small table in his cell and uncovered the basket Blessing had brought, he found some cured ham, biscuits, grits, eggs, milk and a few dried figs. Brown was truly grateful and prayed a prayer of thanksgiving that revealed his appreciation.

As he ate, Blessing and Brown talked. Blessing told Brown, "This place dates back to colonial days when the family of George and Charles Washington lived around here. In fact, there is a tree down this same street, Washington Street, under which George Washington and his Brother Charles sat to plan the City of Charlestown. They were surveyors in their early years, you know, and used to race their horses up and down the streets. According to the plan, the Main Street is Washington Street, and the cross streets are named after members of the Washington family. So the square, where the red brick Greek Revival Court House with white columns is located at the corner of George and Washington Streets. You can look out of the window and see it if you want to, but I'm sure you will be seeing it soon enough!

Photo credit: Doris N. Starks

"George Washington bought land with some of his first earnings as a surveyor down by Bullskin Creek, which is near here. It was about 1,459 acres and some people call it his 'Lost Plantation' because little is mentioned about it, as compared to Mount Vernon. After he bought that land, he persuaded many of his relatives to move here.

"There are also five mansions around here that belong to various members of the Washington family. And more of them are buried here in Zion Episcopal Church's churchyard than are buried at Mount Vernon. I guess you could say that this little old place is full of history. There are a lot of Washingtons still around here.

"Matter of fact, somebody told me you captured Colonel Lewis Washington, a Great- Grand-Nephew of George Washington. Is that true? Did you get the sword from him that once belonged to George Washington? They say it was a gift from Frederick the Great! And how about those pistols he got from Marquis de Lafayette?"

"Not saying whether I did or not, but you can see who is in jail, and it is not Colonel Washington!! But thanks anyway for the information about Charlestown."

Blessing continued, "I kind of love living here in the Upper Shenandoah Valley in the region of the Upper Potomac. Don't know if you are aware of it or not, but *'Shenandoah'* is an Indian word which means 'Daughter of the Stars.' The air feels and smells clean. Where you were a day or two ago around Harpers Ferry is where the Potomac and Shenandoah Rivers meet. That's truly God's country, isn't it? The mountains and the water just make you feel like you're almost in heaven! But I guess that's not the kind of talk you want to hear!"

"You don't have to spare my feelings! If this is my last day of life, I've spent it like I think my God would have me live it. I've done my best not just for myself and my family, but for my fellow-man of all colors and all stations in life, whether in chains or free. I hardly had time to look around in Harpers Ferry. But I'll take your word for it. If I ever get back there, without a noose around my neck, I'll be sure and look around! But I don't think they will show me much hospitality!"

Shortly thereafter, John Blessing left, saying that he had work to do, but would return in the evening, with more food. Brown thanked him again, effusively, and looked forward to Blessing's return. Within his heart, Brown knew that indeed, John Blessing was a blessing from God.

"Give us this day our daily bread...."

After lying on his bed for a while and letting his food digest, Brown got up and took a look out onto the main street. There was a sense of excitement as people moved back and forth up and down the street. Some people were dressed in finer clothes than others. He assumed that the finer dressed people were out-of-towners who had been drawn to Charlestown because of his upcoming trial. There were some who seemed to be writing on note pads, and still others who were drawing pictures of the Courthouse and the jail. He was sure that some were from the local newspaper, the *Spirit of Jefferson,* and *Harper's Weekly* would not miss an opportunity to have a reporter present for his trial. If you asked him, it was more like a preparation for a circus, not a proper discussion of freedom and slavery.

And forgive us our debts,
as we forgive our debtors."

Brown also read other parts of the Bible for comfort and inspiration. Recently he read the scriptures related to John the Baptist. He, too, preached what he believed, and it got him into trouble. And just like The Baptist, Brown might likely lose his own head! So John Brown felt a certain kinship with John the Baptist. At least this story gave him some of the strength he needed to stand up for a cause in which he sincerely believed.

The weather-worn, battle weary man thought of the experience that led him down the path to become an abolitionist. He recalled that when he was only 12 years old his father, Owen Brown, sent him on a cattle drive to take a herd of cattle from Ohio to Michigan. The cows were intended to feed the U. S. Army during the winter of 1812. That was quite a task for a 12 year old boy.

During the cattle drive, Brown stopped along the way with a slave holder who fed him and helped him with the cattle. However, Brown observed that his host, the slave holder, had a slave boy who was approximately the same age as Brown that he treated in an entirely different manner. The slave child could not eat at the table, was poorly fed and clothed, slept in the barn, and was frequently hit with a shovel or whatever was at hand. Further, the child had no parents and suffered in the cold Michigan winter. After that experience, John Brown vowed to devote his life to fight such an evil system.

The next day Brown was visited by his lawyers. They were concerned about how they could best defend him against the charges which had been lodged against him, with the major one being treason. They had with them the report of the incident from Colonel Robert E. Lee who commanded the U. S. Marines that confronted Brown and his men at Harpers Ferry and captured or killed some of them. The lawyers wanted to know what drove Brown to commit such an act and what he hoped to achieve. Brown told them, "I know, and you know that slavery is wrong. It was not my intent to cause a lot of bloodshed. I only wanted to free those who were being held in bondage so they could have a free state here in the Appalachians. I hoped that other Blacks would join the rebellion as it grew. Only those who resisted or posed a danger to the liberators would be in danger of losing their lives. I guess I underestimated the extent to which people would go to protect their valuable *property*."

The lawyers let Brown know that theirs was an almost impossible task, but they would do their best to save his life. They acknowledged that the question of slavery was one that the country needed to settle, but had not yet found a way. They also intimated that they were worried that some of his northern friends might try to organize a rescue party for him, and there would be further bloodshed.

Brown thought that although these men might be well-intentioned, they were between the devil and the deep blue sea. They might want to save his life, but if they did so, they still had to live with their clamoring neighbors who would punish them for their legal efforts on his behalf. Some of the lawyers tried their very best to get Brown to allow them to plead that he was insane. But Brown reasoned that from his point of view, who was more insane, one who tried to set his fellow-man free, or one who was doing all he could to keep him in chains? The bottom line was he could not expect much from his legal team.

Kennedy Farmhouse

After the lawyers left, Brown thought about the plans he had made for his raid. Where had he gone wrong? Did he make a mistake in telling Frederick Douglass, Martin Delany, and some of the "Group of Six" about his plans to raid Harpers Ferry? Did Douglass persuade so many Blacks to refrain from joining the raid that it failed? Although he had received many rifles and 950 pikes from supporters, only 21 men were available for the raid, with three of them left behind at the Kennedy Farmhouse on the actual day of the raid. Perhaps he should have called it off when he did not have the expected numbers to pull off the mission successfully. Maybe he had waited too long for the wagon load of guns to arrive from the Kennedy House. When they did not arrive by the time he expected, perhaps he should have abandoned the mission. What could have kept Charles Tidd and Osborne Anderson so long? Was his base of operations at the Kennedy House too far away? It was in Sharpsburg, Maryland, 7 miles from Harpers Ferry.

There were 18 men in Brown's raiding party. Five were Black and 13 were Caucasian. The Black men were trying to secure freedom for themselves and their families, and both Black and White believed that enslaving human beings was a sin.

Brown remembered that his intention was to take over the Armory in Harpers Ferry so that he could take enough armaments from the Federal Armory to support his cause. After stopping the train that was headed to Baltimore and firing shots that killed the free Black Baggage Master, Hayward Shepherd, perhaps he should not have allowed the train to continue. Then the train's conductor would not have been able to alert the authorities, who then were able to call out the marines.

Photo credit: Doris N. Starks

The Armory at Harpers Ferry had been established by George Washington, and held many armaments for the country's defense. At the time of the raid it held 100,000 muskets and rifles in several buildings. It was Brown's goal to take as many armaments as needed and issue them to slaves to protect themselves as they headed for freedom. However, his co-conspirators were unable to seize the weapons, although there was only one man guarding the Armory on the night of the raid. Instead, they were hemmed up in the Engine House of the Armory Complex by the Marines, and were eventually captured after some were killed and others wounded.

Inside the Engine House, Brown had done all he could to reassure the hostages that his raiders had captured that he meant them no harm. Actually, neither he nor his men hurt them and provided the captives necessities as best they could. It was the moaning and groaning of the wounded raiders that got to Brown the most. Perhaps he just wasn't as strong as he thought.

There were all kinds of "what ifs" that he would do differently if he could plan the raid again. But that was all water under the bridge. Just like water from the Potomac which had already been mixed with that of the Shenandoah in Harpers Ferry, it could not be unmixed.

Brown was held in jail for a month, and his trial began on October 27th. He was still weak from the wounds he sustained at Harpers Ferry and from being in jail. There just was not enough room for him to stretch his long legs adequately.

The prisoner was almost glad to be able to go outside when time came for him to move across the street from the jail and go to the Court House for his trial. In consideration of his health, he was allowed to lie on a cot in the courtroom and give his testimony from that vantage point. Brown sometimes looked at the wall to avoid the angry stares of many in the court room. He was sure that some of them had a right to be angry with him.

The jury consisted of 12 slave holders who deliberated only 45 minutes to determine that Brown was guilty of Treason, Murder, and Insurrection.

"And lead us not into temptation,
but deliver us from evil...."

When John Blessing came to bring him food one evening, he told Brown that the well-known actor, John Wilkes Booth, was in town and was making presentations at the Episcopal Lecture Room on the corner of Lawrence and Liberty streets. Brown thought it quite odd that such a renowned actor would be in such a place as this.

One day Brown rehearsed, with Blessing as his audience, a speech that he planned to make in court. It read, in part, "This court acknowledges, as I suppose, the validity of the law of God. I see a book kissed here which I suppose to be the Bible, or at least the New Testament. That teaches me that all things whatsoever I would that men should do to me, I should do even so to them. It teaches me, further, to 'remember them that are in bonds, as bound with them.' I have endeavored to act up to that instruction. I say, I am yet too young to understand that God is any respecter of persons. I believe that to have interfered as I have done as I have freely admitted I have done in behalf of His despised poor, was not wrong, but right. Now, if it is deemed necessary that I should forfeit my life for the furtherance of the ends of justice, and mingle my blood further with the blood of my children and with the blood of millions in this slave country whose rights are disregarded by wicked, cruel, and unjust enactments, I submit; so let it be done!"

Blessing listened intently, but could not say whether the presentation was good or bad. It was just a sad situation. He had become fond of the man with the long beard and knew what he was saying. Blessing knew how the whole saga would end.

During the trial John Brown listened as the Prosecutor read from the proposed Constitution for the new state in the mountains that was to be populated by former slaves. The document had much in common with the Constitution of the United States of America.

When it became obvious that the president of the new jurisdiction would be "Black", on-lookers at the trial laughed and guffawed loudly and slapped each other's backs so much they had to be reminded by the judge that this was a serious matter and that they needed to treat it as such.

Brown thought the whole thing was rather curious. They behaved like his document had declared something like, "Jesus was Black!" Now that would have really upset them! But come to think of it, would Jesus' Heavenly Father have put Him in that hot environment without any natural protection? No curly hair to allow the heat to help his brain to stay cool? No melanin in His skin to help protect His skin from the hot sun? If He had not been suited for the climate He could not have walked from village to village teaching people. Not only that, the Bible says in the Book of Revelation that His hair was like "Lamb's Wool".

Jesus would have been most miserable in the middle of the desert with European features. Furthermore, it would have been difficult for the Holy Family to hide in the Land of Egypt until it was safe to return home if they had fair skin. Brown imagined Jesus walking from village to village, visiting with friends, such as Lazarus and his sisters, Mary and Martha, in Bethany, just outside Jerusalem. He spoke Aramaic, which was a commonly spoken branch of the Semitic languages.

Brown decided that it was not Jesus' skin tone, language, hair texture, or wealth that mattered. Jesus and all humans are created in God's image, with God's love. Everyone should be treated with love and respect. Therefore, enslavement of another is not part of God's plan.

Judge Richard Parker had a different idea on good and evil. In his Charge to the Jury, Judge Parker said that the accused raiders were "being moved and seduced by the devil!" Maybe one's true answer depended on whether he was in bondage or free.

As the trial approached its close, Brown was asked if he would like to see a minister. He declined the offer. He thought that those who called themselves ministers were likely 'slave-owning hypocrites.' Instead, he considered John Blessing more of a minister to him because Blessing tried to meet both his physical and spiritual needs. Because of the friendship that had developed between the two men, he decided to leave Blessing one of his few worldly possessions. He inscribed his name in his beloved Bible, and gave it to him on his last visit.

Brown wondered how his family would fare during the upcoming Christmas season that was approaching fast. He hoped his wife, Mary Ann, would still make his favorite fruit cake, with fruits she had preserved, although he would not be there to sit around the fire and enjoy it.

In addition to writing a letter to his wife, he also had to write a will for her to handle. That was a harder task. He knew that his family loved him, and he loved them more than they could ever know. But there were some things that required a man to stand up and be counted. He hoped to see them again on the other side where he might be better able to explain himself, that is, with God's help. Until then, he prayed that they would understand and that God would watch over them, and that his life would not be in vain.

Brown prayed further that those he sought to liberate would understand why he undertook his actions and that he wanted them to live in freedom with all of the rights and responsibilities that anyone else had. He sent his love to them over the ages, and hoped they would not forget his sacrifice. Maybe someone else could take up where he left off, perhaps with another tactic, in a new way.

"Lead us not into temptation....."

On December 1st, Mrs. Mary Ann Brown arrived from New York and the couple were so glad to see each other. It was a bittersweet reunion. John was under the impression that she would be staying for the night, but when his request for her to stay was denied he lost his composure. Was there no decency or compassion in these slave-holders? This was the first time he had lost his bearing during his imprisonment. If only he could have held Mary Ann in his arms one last time to tell her how much he loved her and to express his regret at the loss of their two sons, Oliver and Watson, in the raid at Harpers Ferry.

The next day, before leaving his cell for the trial, Brown wrote a note and gave it to his jailer. It read, "I, John Brown, am now quite certain that the crimes of this guilty land will never be purged away but with blood." Brown also gave the jailer his watch.

At around 11 O'clock AM on December 2, 1859, John Brown was found guilty of murdering five persons, conspiring with slaves to rebel, and with treason against the State of Virginia. He was then led out of the Court House, with his arms tied. There were many people crowded around him and his handlers.

As Brown reached the street, a barefoot Black woman wearing a tattered dress with a red bandana around her hair pushed her way to the front of the crowd. She was holding her young child in front of her. She tearfully asked Brown to kiss and bless the child. Although it was obvious that Brown had many problems of his own, he complied with the woman's request and kissed her baby gently and from his eyes came a blessing. He was then pushed toward the waiting wagon.

One of the two horses was white and called "Daisy" by the man on the front seat holding the horses' reins. Daisy seemed to sense that she was being forced to take part in something that was not in agreement with her nature and spirit. She wanted to run away, but the man was holding her reins tightly. Maybe it was her maternal instinct which told her that the pitiful creature with his arms tied was in some kind of trouble. But if he was such a bad man, why did the woman hold her baby up to him? Surely the baby was the most precious thing the bedraggled woman had! And was that some king of tangled rope around his neck? No one else coming out of the building had a rope around his neck!

Daisy focused her large eyes with the big eyelashes on the man with the long beard as men brought him toward the wagon. There was such disgust in the men's eyes! What had the bearded man done to cause the other men to regard him with such disdain? He had to be in some kind of trouble.

Oh, well, the bearded man's arms were bound, and he couldn't do anything now. Not only that, but he did not have on enough clothes for the cold weather. Daisy felt sorry for him and tears welled up in her eyes. After he was loaded onto the wagon, and the men made him sit on the big black, coffin-looking box, Daisy decided that the only help she could give this poor, wretched man was for her to walk carefully wherever they were taking him. She would avoid as many mud holes and pot holes as she could to make his ride as smooth as possible.

"Deliver us from evil ....."

Zion Episcopal Church

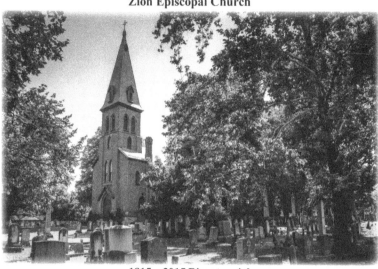

1815 – 2015 Bicentennial

Photo Credit: Thom Potts

On the command of the horses' driver, Daisy pulled away from the Courthouse, then maneuvered across Washington Street onto Samuel Street giving guidance to the other horse to follow her. As the entourage continued along Samuel Street the clip-clop of the horses' hooves sounded mournful as if they were counting Brown's last moments on the face of the earth. He would surely be dead within the hour - just as dead as the souls in nearby Zion Episcopal Church's cemetery.

As the chill December wind blew through his clothes, Brown coughed. He thought that if this question of slavery was not solved soon, it would tear the nation apart, just as his coughing felt like it was tearing his chest apart, muscle from muscle and nerve from nerve.

Or maybe he was already dead! Did anyone else see those two gauzy, ethereal men marching alongside the wagon? The one at the front-left side of the wagon looked like his long-dead father, Owen Brown. And who was the man at the front right? No, it couldn't be! His attire was certainly not from around here. He had on some type of hairy outfit that was cinched around his middle with an animal skin belt. His hair looked uncombed and he also had a beard. Could it really be John the Baptist? The two marchers were unnoticed by other men around the wagon. Also, the two shimmery marchers had such a regal bearing it seemed like they were escorting a chariot, not an old wagon!! *Hallelujah!!*

"For thine is the kingdom..."

Brown said nothing, but listened to the rhythmic beat of the horses' hooves. When the driver finally said, "Whoa," Daisy knew she had reached her destination. She had done her best for the pitiful man. Daisy's was the last act of mercy shown to John Brown on Samuel Street.

As he was led onto the hanging grounds, Brown noticed more than 80 cadets from Virginia Military Institute under the command of Major Thomas J. Jackson (later known as

"Stonewall") and faculty member William Gilham from Virginia Military Institute. They had with them two howitzers. It was an impressive sight. Why such a display of power? Were they expecting a last-minute rescue attempt by his northern friends?

"And the power, and the glory...."

Scene from the Hanging of John Brown in 1859, showing VMI Cadet Guard; from VMI Archives

Although Brown did not know it, John Wilkes Booth was also in the hanging area, wearing a VMI uniform as a disguise. He even wore a red flannel shirt like the other cadets. Booth just could not bear being unable to watch and testify to the proceedings about to take place. He thought, "How could this unspeakable, gaunt character have tried to pull off a slave rebellion? What are his values? He is certainly no gentleman!"

As Brown surveyed the crowd, he thought to himself, "What could they possibly be teaching these young men? How can they afford to outfit them in such handsome outfits to bring them here to see me hanged? Surely my friends, Henry David Thoreau and Ralph Waldo Emerson, would say that the faculty should find something better for them to do. Those in charge of these cadets will have to give an account to a higher authority for this."

Even then Brown's abiding thought was that his beloved country was bearing a heavy burden because of slavery. It would hold them back and prevent their progress if they did not deal with it at once! It would be as if these fine young cadets would be given a command of "Forward, March!!", but then each one would plant one foot firmly on the other. There could not and would not be any progress if many of the nation's people were prevented from being citizens, were enslaved, and kept from reaching their full potential. It was so sad that the slave holders could not see that.

"Forever..."

As the white hood was lowered over his head and face, John Brown commended his soul to his Heavenly Father. In his remaining moments of life, Brown sent his love forward to generations of Americans, hoping they would be able to live together in peace and harmony, regarding each other as brothers and sisters, in the spirit of Divine Love. But scenes of men in blue and gray uniforms with guns, fighting each other flashed before his eyes! He even thought he heard thunderous booms of canons! Maybe it was just thunder...

He then felt the executioner cut the rope that had been attached to the onerous noose around his neck. The floor beneath Brown gave way and he fell through the trap door beneath him.

As Brown's body fell through the trap door, his *true* self was caught and embraced by Jesus. Brown recognized Him because He was as Brown had imagined Him to be. He had hair like "lamb's wool," and his skin had an awesome glowing tint, with just the right amount of melanin. Jesus whispered into the ear of a shocked and joyful John Brown, "We're going home!"

The hanging grounds faded in the background as Jesus and John Brown rose heavenward.

"Amen!!" So Be It!!

ABOUT THE AUTHOR

In addition to being a writer of short stories and other professional materials, Dr. Doris N. Starks has had a career in Nursing Education Administration. Her last appointment was that of Dean and Professor of Nursing, as well as Founding Director of the Community Health Center at Coppin State University in Baltimore.

Dr. Starks has also been on the faculties and leadership teams at Tuskegee University and Baltimore City Community College Schools of Nursing.

Among her many interests, Dr. Starks includes History and Social Justice. She currently votes in the court room of the Jefferson County Court House in Charles Town, West Virginia, where John Brown was tried for treason.

Before relocating to Charles Town, Dr. Starks lived with her family in Columbia, Maryland, and Tuskegee, Alabama.

In the story, the city is called *Charlestown, Virginia.* It was not known as Charles Town, West Virginia, until after the Civil War.

Oil painting on the cover is, "The Last Moments of John Brown" by Thomas Hovenden.

DEDICATION

This story is dedicated to my family; husband Wilbert, Sr., sons Wilbert, Jr., (Bert) and Garrick.

It is also dedicated to the memory of James Alvin Tolbert, Sr. and his family.

James Alvin Tolbert, Sr. was a devoted husband to his wife, Shirley, and their sons, James, Jr., Michael, and Stephen.

Tolbert was a well-known advocate for Civil Rights and Social Justice in West Virginia and other areas. He worked by assuming leadership roles in the National Association for the Advancement of Colored People at the local, state and regional levels. He collaborated with other community organizations to empower people and provide them with needed services.

Lifelong membership at St. Philip Episcopal Church in Charles Town gave Tolbert an opportunity to demonstrate his strong religious faith. In addition to membership at St. Philip, Tolbert was a member of Prince Hall Grand Lodge of West Virginia, and a member of Alpha Phi Alpha Fraternity. He served on the boards of many civic and community organizations; he had a talent for working with others to achieve common goals that were in the community's best interest.

Tolbert was also dedicated to preserving and restoring buildings and items that were relevant to African American History. He was truly a "Servant Leader."

POSTSCRIPT

The American Civil War began in 1861, two years after the hanging of John Brown in 1859. The primary issue that propelled the nation toward war was slavery. There were approximately 620,000 deaths among both the Northern (blue) and Southern (gray) states.

Was Brown a domestic terrorist, or was he, as he saw it, trying to abolish the "sin of slavery" in America? The debate continues.

RESOURCES ON JOHN BROWN AND THE RAID ON HARPERS FERRY CAN BE FOUND IN WEST VIRGINIA ARCHIVES AND HISTORY.

CPSIA information can be obtained
at www.ICGtesting.com
Printed in the USA
LVHW071913110820
662820LV00038B/234/J